# Love to Jaixai and Vonchai, From Laos

## (A Laotian Tapestry of Stories, Recipes and Love)

Written by: Dengnoi Reineke
Illustrated by: Ruslan Skomohorov

*To Josh – my love,*
*and Jaixai - my life, my muse.*
*~Noi*

**To my parents,**
**Valentina and Sergey,**
**who always supported me.**
**~Ruslan**

"Bong! Bong! Bong!" the drums sound in the distance.

"It is time to wake up, Jaixai," her mother smoothes her hair away from her face.

Jaixai stretches her arms up in the air and breathes in the fresh smell of rice cooking outside on the kitchen fire.

It is still dark, but there is much to do before dawn.

Every morning, Jaixai has a special duty. She climbs up the banana tree and breaks off a few big leaves. Momma will use them to wrap her delicious rice treats. From the top of the tree, she waves to her friends, Joshi and Ling monkey.

"I think this is a good one," Joshi yells from across the trees. He holds up a young coconut. Just then, Ling monkey snatches it from Joshi's hand and scampers happily down the trunk with his confiscated prize.

Jaixai laughs at Ling monkey, and climbs down with two big banana leaves for momma. She helps momma arrange the sweet offerings of treats on a bamboo-woven platter.

The sun starts to slowly
stretch its arms up in a big
yawn, over the mountains.
Silhouettes of crimson gold waves
can be seen approaching the village.
The drums sound louder.

"*Sabaidee*\*, Jaixai," an elderly neighbor greets her, showing
off her teeth, stained red from chewing betel leaves. Today,
the neighbor has marigolds and mangoes picked from her garden.

"Sabaidee. How is your health today?" Jaixai asks.

The neighbor smiles and addresses momma, "Jai is getting to
be a fine young lady."

Jaixai stands up straight and tall, like a big girl. She feels proud
and responsible next to her momma, giving tithes to the monks.
Soon all of the neighbors exchange morning greetings.

\**Sabaidee*: Hello

"The Buddhist monks are approaching," momma says.

The monks are in a straight line, each one carrying a wide, wooden vase. The monk in front starts playing the *khaen*, a traditional Laotian instrument.

As they march slowly by, Jaixai and momma place their offerings into each of their wooden vase. Each time, momma whispers a little wish of health and happiness for loved ones, living and past.

Then the drums and the sound of the khaen fade away, as the monks continue on their journey, back to the temple in the mountains above the village.

While everyone scatters to have breakfast or go to the rice fields, Jaixai remains standing at the front of the house. She enjoys watching the crimson sea fade into the distance, giving a splash of color to the green fields that seem to stretch for miles.

After the morning routine, Jaixai gets a ride on Grandfather's bike to the rice paddies.

Daddy waves to them from under his sun hat. It is wet season, so daddy is busy planting the young rice plants.

As Jaixai approaches him, she begs, "Daddy, please, please, please!"

"Oh, alright," daddy laughs. He takes his work gloves off and lifts Jaixai up on the water ox.
Grandfather has started planting a new row. He motions with his hands, "Come, child."

He holds up a tiny black water snake.

"He will not harm you. He is good for the crops because he will keep the mice away," Grandfather explains.

Jaixai holds the snake and it tickles her hands as it slips back into the water. Soon they are all singing and planting.

At noon, they share a meal of fried rice and a salad of jackfruit and rambutan.

"Momma, I saw a water snake and he was harmless and he means good luck for our crops!" Jaixai exclaims. Momma smiles and pulls up a chair.

"Would you like to work at the loom today?"

"Oh, momma! Oh, momma! *Kop chai*\*!" She embraces her mom.

Jaixai has always wanted to learn the art of weaving, a craftsmanship that has been passed down for many generations among the women in her family. One day, she too will have the honor and privilege to teach her daughter.

As momma patiently guides Jaixai's little hands, she chants a poem,

> "In and out, life and love
> through and through
> health and happiness, peace and joy
> passion for what you do."

Momma has a soft, pretty voice. Jai is at ease at the loom.

\**Kop Chai*: Thank you

Grandmother chants along with momma.

"Red and black, green and gold
Weave the threads of life
Silver, pink, blue and brown
Colors of the earth and sky."

9

The night air is cool and there is a full moon out. Tonight, Grandmother will wash Jaixai's hair in the moonlight.

"Come, child."

Jaixai lays straight across the wooden bench and lets her long, brown hair fall off the edge.

Grandmother pours the warm coconut milk on her hair.

"Please tell me the story about the Lotus Princess."

As her hands massage Jaixai's hair, Grandmother begins her evening ritual of story telling...

\* \* \*

Once upon a time in *bahn*\* Nakkhounnoi there lived a little girl, Vonchai, and her grandparents. One day while Vonchai was gathering water chestnuts, she met a woman who wanted to take her away.

"Please, do not take Vonchai. We will repay our debts to you in full, as soon as we can. Please, have mercy on us for we are old and we have nothing, but our granddaughter to live for," the grandparents pleaded with the woman.

The cunning woman finally said, "I will return for the next three days. Each day, you must provide an offering to me that I will request in a clue. If on the third day, you have succeeded, your debts will be forgiven and you shall never see me again. However, if you guess wrong, even once, then I will take Vonchai as my servant."

The grandparents had no choice, but to accept this unkind woman's proposition. They will go to the temple tonight and seek wisdom.

\**Bahn*: Village

The first night, Vonchai's grandparents dutifully climbed up the mountain to the little *Wat**.

The Buddhist monk only said, "Trust in the strength of your love for Vonchai."

Although they left the temple with no foresight as to what the unkind woman may request tomorrow, they were enlightened. The Ah Chan's chants fulfilled their hearts with warmth and hope.

The next day, the woman returned and requested, "Although some may consider this fruit's smell very pungent, I consider it an aphrodisiac. It is the king of the fruit that I so desire."

The elderly couple answered with a smile. "It is the durian fruit that you so desire."

All of the villagers were gathered around to assist the poor, elderly couple.

One of the villagers offered, "So, it is the durian *mak mai**  that you shall have." He handed to her a sweet durian fruit from his garden.

All the villagers chanted in chorus, "It takes a village to raise a child!"

*Wat: Temple
*Mak mai: Fruit

12

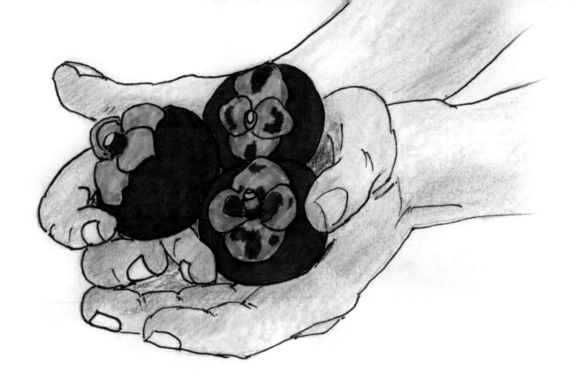

The second night, Vonchai's grandparents dutifully climbed up the mountain to the little temple to seek wisdom. This time the Ah Chan said, "Trust in the strength of your neighbors' love for the child."

And again, although they left the temple with no foresight as to what the unkind woman may request tomorrow, they were still enlightened. The Buddhist monk's chants fulfilled their hearts with warmth and hope.

The second day, the woman returned with a bigger smile and requested, "Yesterday, I had the king of fruit. Today, it is the queen of the mak mai that I so desire."

The elderly couple did not have an answer. Again, all of the villagers were gathered around to assist the poor, elderly couple. "It is the mangosteen fruit that you so desire," one of their kind neighbors finally responded.

Another villager offered, "So, it is the mangosteen fruit that you shall have." She handed to the unkind woman the mangosteen fruit from her garden.

All the villagers chanted in chorus, "It takes a village to raise a child!"

For two days now, the elderly couple managed to offer the woman what she wanted. However, they were still fearful that tomorrow they may not be able to provide for the woman's desire. They may never see Vonchai again.

Dutifully, Vonchai's grandparents climbed up the mountain to the little Wat to seek wisdom. As dawn was approaching, the couple was tired and decided to return to their bahn. As they were about to leave, the Buddhist monk interrupted his chant.

This time he calmly said to them, "Your love for Vonchai is pure. Trust also in the strength of Vonchai's love for you." With those words, Vonchai's grandparents left the temple with enlightened minds and hearts.

The third day, the woman returned. This time she had gifts of palm seeds.

"These palm seeds shall be for you, for you will need something sweet to ease your pain when I take Vonchai away!" the woman laughed.

The woman requested, "I crave this mak mai. Others may deem it a flower."

The elderly couple was puzzled. They did not have an answer. They looked to the villagers who gathered around the third day as well. There was silence.

"So, give me an answer and be quick with it!" the unkind woman demanded.

The elderly couple begged her again for mercy, for they had no idea what the answer could possibly be. Then a small voice was heard, "I shall provide what it is that you so desire."

Everyone looked around, wondering where the voice was coming from. "It is me," the voice said. "Over here."

"Where are you? *U-sai*\*? *U-sai* ? " the woman demanded in frustration. She had very little patience.

"I am here. I am the lotus plant, a plant bestowed with the nature of flower and fruit. I am Vonchai."

The villagers turned to the direction of the pond and saw the single tall lotus plant.

\**U-sai*: Where?

Because Vonchai's love for her grandparents was very pure, the young child returned her grandparents' unconditional love in a magical way.

The woman threw the palm seeds on the ground and ran off in fear. She believed that an evil curse would eventually strike her down for her unkind ways. She never returned to bahn Nakkhounnoi.

Vonchai turned back into a little girl and ran to hug her grandparents and the other villagers who were so generous and kind.

All of the villagers cheered and chanted in unison at the running woman, "It takes a village to raise a child!"

* * *

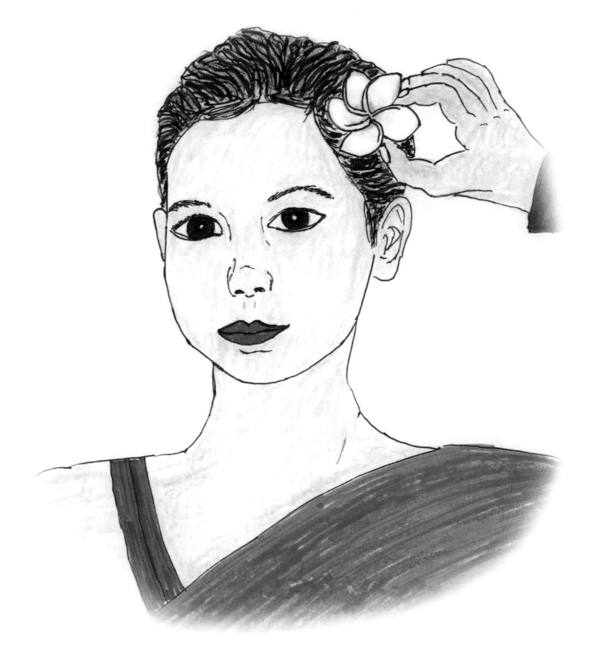

Grandmother finishes up washing Jaixai's hair with the warm, kaffir lime juice. Afterwards, she places a *dok champa* flower in the child's hair.

Jaixai sleepily whispers, "*Koy huk chou lai*\*."

## THE END

\**Koy huk chou lai*: I love you very much

# Recipes

| | Sweet Sticky Rice Treat (serving: 4-6) |
|---|---|
| *1 cup Black Thai sticky rice<br><br>*1 cup Thai sticky rice<br><br>*2 cups canned unsweetened coconut milk<br><br>*1/4 cup palm sugar or brown sugar<br><br>*1 good size taro (2 cups when chopped into bite-sized cubes) | **Step #1:** Soak the Black Thai sticky rice and the Thai sticky rice together in plenty of water for 24 hours. Drain.<br><br>**Step #2:** Peel bark off taro root. Wash. Chop into bite-sized cubes.<br><br>**Step #3:** Steam taro until soft. Set aside to cool.<br><br>**Step #4:** Place rice in a cheesecloth-lined steamer or a large bamboo sieve. Set steamer in a saucepan of water, cover and bring to a boil. Steam for 30 minutes. Occasionally use wet, wooden spoon to gently stir. Set aside to cool.<br><br>**Step #5:** Warm coconut milk and palm sugar over low heat. Do not bring to boil.<br><br>**Step #6:** Place cooked rice into a bowl. Add taro. Slowly pour in warm coconut milk, while using a wet wooden spoon to gently stir into rice and taro. Cover loosely with plastic wrap. Set aside for 3-4 hours.<br><br>Serve in a small bowl. |

|  |  |
|---|---|
| *2 cups Longan fruit<br><br>*1 1/2 cups soymilk<br><br>*2 scoops vanilla ice cream<br><br>*1/2 cup black tapioca pearls | **<u>Longan Smoothie (serving: 2)</u>**<br><br>Step #1:  Boil black tapioca pearls in 4-5 cups of water until soft (15-25 minutes)<br><br>Step #2:  Wash tapioca pearls in cold water.  Drain.<br><br>Step #3:  Remove seeds from longan<br><br>Step #4:  Puree in blender longan, soymilk and vanilla ice cream.  Pour into glass.<br><br>Step #5:  Stir in tapioca pearls<br><br>Enjoy!  [fruit alternatives:  Rambutan, Mangosteen, Jackfruit, Mango] |

|  |  |
|---|---|
| *2 cups Water Chestnuts<br><br>*1 cup raspberries<br><br>*1 avocado<br><br>*2 mangoes<br><br>*2 pomegranates<br><br>*1 cup crushed, roasted walnuts | **<u>Water Chestnut Salad (serving: 2-3)</u>**<br><br>Step #1:  Wash and drain water chestnuts and raspberries<br><br>Step #2:  Prepare and chop avocado, mangoes, pomegranates<br><br>Step #3:  Toss ingredients into salad bowl<br><br>Step #4:  Sprinkle roasted walnuts<br><br>Serve with dressing of your choice on the side (fruity dressing is recommended, such as raspberry vinaigrette) |

| | |
|---|---|
| *1 cup small tapioca pearls<br><br>*1 good size taro (2 cups when chopped into bite-sized cubes)<br><br>*1 ¾ cups coconut milk<br><br>*1/2 cup palm sugar<br><br>*1/2 cup brown sugar | **<u>Taro & Tapioca Pudding (serving: 4-6)</u>**<br><br>Step #1:  Boil 6 cups of water.  Add tapioca pearls to boiling water for 15-20 minutes.  Drain under cold water.<br><br>Step #2:  Peel bark off taro root.  Wash.  Chop into bite-sized cubes.<br><br>Step #3:  Steam taro until soft.  Set aside to cool.<br><br>Step #4:  Warm coconut milk, palm sugar and brown sugar over low heat.  Do not bring to boil.<br><br>Step #5:  Stir in tapioca pearls and taro.  Sprinkle on fresh nutmeg and cinnamon.<br><br>Enjoy hot or cold.  (This dessert is delicious chilled over night!) |

| | |
|---|---|
| *4-5 Kaffir Limes | **<u>Kaffir Lime Conditioner</u>**<br><br>Step #1:  Squeeze juice from kaffir limes, either by hand or with juicer<br><br>Step #2:  Heat kaffir lime juice over low heat.  Do not bring to boil.<br><br>Step #3:  Gently massage the warm kaffir lime juice on wet, shampooed hair and scalp.  (Make sure the juice is warm to touch and does not burn scalp.)<br><br>Step #4:  Leave on for 2-3 minutes.  Thoroughly rinse with warm water.<br><br>This wonderful and aromatic conditioner will leave hair very silky! |

# Author

Dengnoi Reineke graduated from Brown University with a B.A. in International Relations (2001) and M.A. in Development Studies (2005). Noi has lived and traveled extensively throughout Asia, Europe and Central America. She has served as an international consultant for the Laotian Ministry of Education, the United Nations Save the Children Organization, the Vocational Cambodian Center for the Disabled in Cambodia, the Asian Development Bank and the Ministry of International Relations in South Korea. She currently is a consultant for an investment firm and a foundation based in Washington, D.C.

Whenever she got ill as a young girl in bahn Nakkhounnoi, her grandfather barbecued gecko for her to eat because he believed it would help cure her.

Noi resides in Michigan with her husband, Dr. Reineke who is a fellow "Brownie", their daughter, Jaixai, and two lovely cats, Sagwa and Snow.

This is her debut children's book.

# Illustrator

Ruslan Skomorohov was born in Dimitrovgrad, Bulgaria in a family of engineers. He went to Brown University on a full scholarship as an international student. Ruslan graduated in 2009 with two degrees - B.S. in Physics and B.A. in Economics. Along with his scientific inclination, Ruslan has an interest for the arts, exploring many disciplines, including painting, photography, graphic design and poetry. He created the design for an aviation and aerospace magazine and multiple posters for advertising campaigns.

He turns into a sweets-eating monster when there are marshmallows, jelly or jellybons around.

This book is his debut as a freelance illustrator.
Please feel free to contact him at ruslan_s_s@yahoo.com.

# GreenSoul Shoes

GreenSoul Shoes is a 100% recycled, waste reducing American shoe company that aims to shoe 300 million shoeless children. The company uses a market-based restoration model that creates an award-winning global marketplace for Third World shoemakers. For every pair of shoes sold, GreenSoul Shoes also gives away a pair to a child in a Third World community. For more information, please visit http://greensoulshoes.wordpress.com.

Stephen Chen is a cofounder of GreenSoul Shoes and holds a B.S. in Biology from Brown University (2004). Stephen has been featured in the NY Times, Wall Street Journal, Washington Post, ABC, NBC and NPR.

4605298

Made in the USA
Charleston, SC
17 February 2010